Too Perfect

by Trudy Ludwig

Illustrated by Lisa Fields

TRICYCLE PRESS
BERKELEY / TORONTO

Have you ever wished you could be somebody else? I have. I wished I was Kayla. Then all my problems would go away like magic. Poof!—No more frizzy hair and freckles. I'd have cool clothes instead of boring hand-me-downs. I'd get straight A's instead of a bunch of B's and C's. I'd be a better me—smarter, thinner, prettier—and I'd have more friends.

Mom always said, "Maisie, you're perfect just the way you are." But she didn't know perfect. She didn't know Kayla.

In class, I watched Kayla all the time.

If I looked hard enough, maybe I'd find the secret to being perfect. Then I'd live happily ever after—just like Kayla.

A few weeks ago, my teacher, Ms. Kim, assigned Kayla to be my science project partner. So on Monday, after school, we got together at Kayla's house to start working on our project.

"What's that?" she asked when she saw the plate I was holding.

"Brownies," I said. "My mom baked them for a study treat. You want one?"

"No thanks. I've already eaten."

While we studied, I ate a brownie. Every time I took a bite, Kayla watched me. "Are you sure you don't want a brownie?" I asked her.

"I already told you, I had a snack," she snapped back. "Besides, my mom says eating sweets makes you fat."

Did Kayla think I was fat? I put my brownie down and didn't take another bite.

On Thursday, Mom dropped me off at Kayla's soccer game
so we could work on our project afterwards.

I watched Kayla run up and down the soccer field. She was
so-o-o fast. If I played like her, I bet those girls would love to
have me on their team.

"Pass the ball!" Kayla shouted at Ana, her teammate.
"Pass it NOW!" Ana did what Kayla told her. But when
Kayla finally kicked the ball, she missed the goal.

"This is *your* fault!" Kayla hissed at Ana. "If you had passed the ball to me sooner, I would've had a perfect shot."

"It's just a game, Kayla. We're supposed to be having fun," said another teammate.

"I'm not here for fun . . . I'm here to win," she replied as she stomped off the field.

"Hey, Kayla," I shouted, running after her, "you were great out there!"

"Not great enough," she mumbled as she looked at her dad.

"But you really tried hard to make that goal . . ."

"What good is trying if you don't win?"

That's when I started to think that being perfect wasn't easy . . . or fun.

On Sunday, Kayla came over so we could finish up our project. Every time she wrote a sentence, she would erase it. "Kayla, what are you doing?" I asked her.

"I'm not happy with the ending. It's not good enough."

I looked over her shoulder. "But I like what you wrote. What's wrong with it?"

"Everything!" she said, crumpling the report in her hands.

"Kayla, stop it!" I yelled as I grabbed the papers from her. "Our report is due tomorrow!"

"You don't understand," said Kayla. And then she started to cry.

I tried to make her feel better, but I wasn't much help. Mom overheard Kayla sniffling and asked her if she was okay.

"I–I'm just coming down with a c–c–cold."

I could tell Mom didn't believe her, but she left us alone anyway.

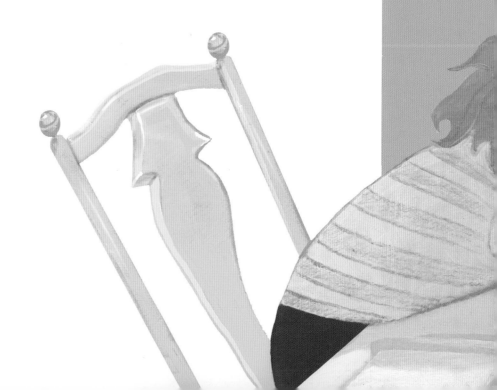

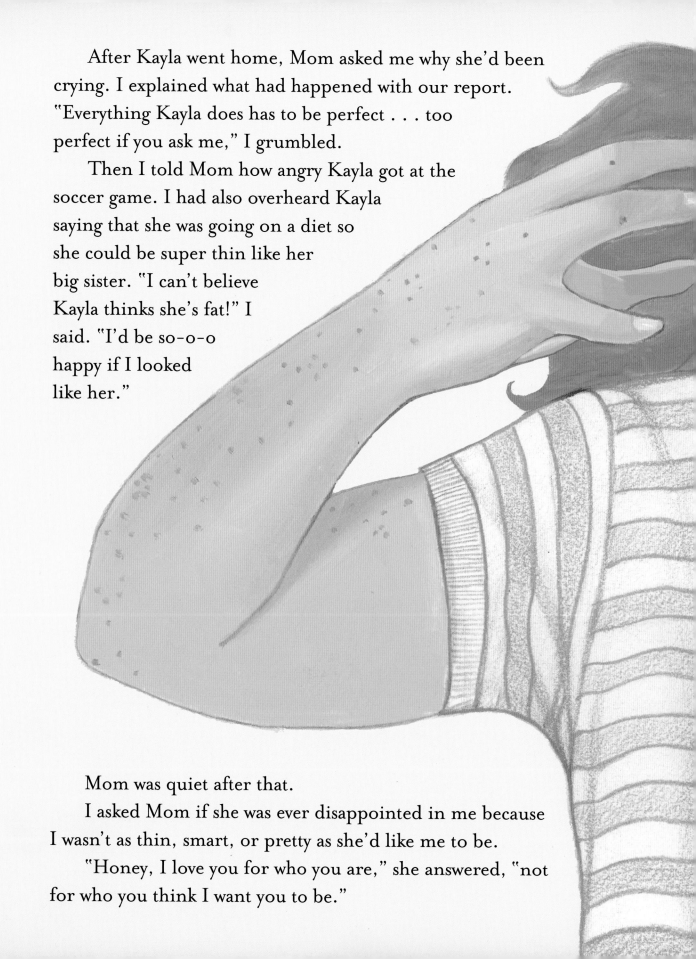

After Kayla went home, Mom asked me why she'd been crying. I explained what had happened with our report. "Everything Kayla does has to be perfect . . . too perfect if you ask me," I grumbled.

Then I told Mom how angry Kayla got at the soccer game. I had also overheard Kayla saying that she was going on a diet so she could be super thin like her big sister. "I can't believe Kayla thinks she's fat!" I said. "I'd be so-o-o happy if I looked like her."

Mom was quiet after that.

I asked Mom if she was ever disappointed in me because I wasn't as thin, smart, or pretty as she'd like me to be.

"Honey, I love you for who you are," she answered, "not for who you think I want you to be."

"Life isn't perfect. We aren't perfect," Mom added, "but by trying new things and learning from our mistakes, we can become better at whatever we choose to do. Maisie, do you remember when you took swimming lessons?"

"Uh-huh. I was scared at first."

"But then the more you practiced,
the stronger you got."
"And now I love to swim," I said.

"Are you happy doing what you love to do?"

"Yeah!"

"Do you know what makes Kayla happy?" Mom asked.

I thought hard about it for a few minutes but I couldn't come up with anything, which really surprised me. Kayla was as close to perfect as anyone I knew, but I couldn't think of one thing that made her happy.

Mom told me that lots of kids—and even grownups—put pressure on themselves or felt pressured by others to act or look a certain way. "Being happy doesn't come from being perfect," she said. "It comes from trusting and accepting who you are— mistakes and all."

On Monday, Kayla didn't come to school. I waited until after class to hand in our report. When Ms. Kim asked me why it was all crumpled, I told her what had happened the night before. Then she asked more questions. I didn't want to answer because I was afraid of getting Kayla in trouble.

"Maisie," said Ms. Kim, "I'm just trying to understand how big of a problem this is for Kayla."

So I told her what I had told my Mom.

"You obviously care about Kayla. Thanks for letting me know," said Ms. Kim. "I'll meet with the school counselor to see what we can do to help Kayla."

When I came home from school that day, I told Mom about my talk with Ms. Kim. She was glad that I had shared my worries with my teacher.

Then Mom suggested we have "Appreciation Time" once a week, where we take turns at the dinner table, saying one thing that we appreciate about each other. "Let's celebrate who we are instead of complaining about who we aren't," she explained.

Appreciation Time has helped me a lot. Hearing my family say how much they appreciate me feels really good. I also like seeing how happy my family and friends are when I tell them what I like and respect about them.

I know that I'm not perfect. But that doesn't mean I can't do good things. Mom says no one can do a better job being Maisie than me. You know what? I think she's right.

Afterword

In Trudy Ludwig's beautifully crafted story, Maisie envies her friend Kayla, a classmate whose world looks perfect. But as Maisie gets to know Kayla better, both she and the reader learn that Kayla's life is anything but enviable. Kayla doesn't seem to be permitted to lose, or to have fun, or to be anything less than perfect. Losers are frowned upon and are not acceptable, and the brief glimpses we get of perceived judgment and disapproval from Kayla's parents hint at the sources of these beliefs. Kayla is trapped.

Too Perfect would make a sufficient point if it were simply an observation about the discouraging and burdensome lives that perfectionists routinely experience. It goes beyond that, though. With impressive succinctness and empathic clarity, Ludwig gives us a glimmer of what it is like to be Kayla. We see a young girl who is talented, energetic, yet profoundly sad and anxious. When Maisie tries to reassure her that she is good enough as she is, Kayla says Maisie doesn't understand. Indeed, to a perfectionist, accepting less-than-perfect is tantamount to admitting that one is a lesser person.

Perfectionism is a burden; it is never healthy. The struggle to be perfect—not just very good but perfect—immerses perfectionists in lives of constant anxiety and self-judgment. The fear of imperfection is overwhelming. It leads, defensively, to chronic pressure to perform and to blame others who might appear to interfere with that performance. Research consistently demonstrates that perfectionism can be a fellow traveler to depression, anxiety, eating disorders, and disturbances in intimacy. The pursuit of excellence, which can certainly involve high motivation, strenuous effort, and critical self-reflection, parts company with perfectionism when the underlying motivations are understood. Perfectionists believe themselves to be what psychologists call conditionally acceptable. Their sense of themselves is that there may be some inherent flaw within them that makes them unacceptable as people and that perhaps, *if* they can be perfect, acceptance will follow. The struggle to be perfect is a constant challenge, and since, in Maisie's mom's words, "Life isn't perfect. We aren't perfect," it is definitely a losing battle.

If perfectionism's wellspring is an emotional conviction that perfection is the road to personal acceptance, then Maisie's mom gives us a key to overcoming it. Her suggestion is so simple and yet so profound: let's make sure we take time to say what we appreciate about each other. That such an idea might seem surprising speaks to a tragic element in our contemporary culture. A winner-take-all, you're-either-first-or-you're-nothing perspective and a hypercompetitive attitude lead naturally to the conclusion that you are either perfect or you are basically worthless. We are quick to say what we don't like and to

offer critiques, but we are not practiced in the art of encouragement, or of simply saying what we like or appreciate about someone. Maisie, in Ludwig's story, seems perceptive, engaged, thoughtful, compassionate, feeling, and brave. Note that none of these qualities involve a product of Maisie's that must be measured or graded. Mom doesn't aim to rate Maisie on her performance; she simply likes her for who she is and decides to tell her that. Perhaps Kayla's parents, who seem supportive of Kayla's talents, can learn to do this as well. If Maisie and Kayla can feel accepted for who they are, then they will feel less need to be perfect. A mistake will be just a mistake, and they can invest energy in being good at things they like to do, without the conviction that only perfect will suffice. What a wonderful relief that will be!

Too Perfect makes us aware of something else crucial to the understanding of perfectionism: Kayla seems to the world to be arrogant, single-minded, and at times angry. What we learn is that she is profoundly sad, anxious, and discouraged. Perfectionism isn't a disease to be conquered; it is a self-esteem issue in need of healing. This book shows us how we might begin to do just that.

THOMAS S. GREENSPON, PhD
Licensed Psychologist
Licensed Marriage and Family Therapist
Author of
Freeing Our Families from Perfectionism
and
*What to Do When Good Enough Isn't Good Enough:
The Real Deal on Perfectionism: A Guide for Kids*

Author's Note:
The Impossible Pursuit of Perfection

*"It is better to live your own destiny imperfectly than to
live an imitation of somebody else's life with perfection."*
—Ancient Indian yogic text paraphrased by
Elizabeth Gilbert, author of *Eat, Pray, Love*

Too Perfect is a story I felt personally and professionally driven to write—personally because I am a recovering perfectionist myself and professionally because experts report that perfectionism is commonplace among adults and children in our society. Our culture's incessant pressure for us to be "the best" in what we do and how we look provides a fertile ground for perfectionism to take root and choke our spirit.

The perfectionist's world is one of unrealistic expectations, harsh disappointments, and brutal extremes. If you're not a winner, you're a loser. If you're not beautiful and thin, you're ugly and fat. If you make mistakes, you've got no hope of succeeding. You are critical of yourself and others. And, as with Kayla in *Too Perfect*, you inevitably reach a point where this all-or-nothing pursuit of perfection takes its toll on your physical and mental well-being. Perfectionists, experts cite, are susceptible to depression, anger, fear, low self-esteem, troubled interpersonal relationships, performance anxiety, procrastination, headaches, gastrointestinal problems, and eating disorders.

Dr. Thomas Greenspon, author of *Freeing Our Families from Perfectionism*, explains

that perfectionism has more to do with "the fear of failure than the urge for success." Ironically, he adds, this very strong fear of making mistakes can actually cause children to miss opportunities for accomplishment and interfere with their ability to do well.

There is nothing wrong with wanting to do our best, explain Miriam Adderholdt, PhD and Jan Goldberg, authors of *Perfectionism: What's Bad About Being Too Good?* But the constant need to be the best is too much of a burden for anyone—especially young children—to bear. In her book *Being Perfect*, Anna Quindlen likens this burden to wearing a backpack filled with bricks. We need to take this burden off our backs, she says, to prevent permanent curvature of the spirit.

Turning Away from Perfection and Striving toward Excellence

How can we help children overcome perfectionism (what they think they *must* do) and strive toward excellence (what they *can* do), in which they set healthier, more reasonable standards and achieve more balance in their lives? Below are some coping strategies perfectionists of all ages can use as a starting point:

— Be kinder and less critical of yourself and others. Nobody is perfect.

— Allow for mistakes; they're an important part of the learning process.

— Take pleasure in what you're doing. Enjoy the journey, not just the destination.

— Don't overcommit yourself. Allow for some personal downtime.

— When you feel overwhelmed, take a break and do something else.

— Focus on your strengths and celebrate your accomplishments.

— Take a risk by trying something new— just for the fun of it.

— If you get stuck, don't be afraid to ask for help.

— If you can't cope, seek the professional help of a counselor or therapist.

For more information about perfectionism, please refer to Recommended Readings.

Questions for Discussion

"I can't believe she thinks she's fat. I'd be so-o-o happy if I looked like her."

Have you ever wanted to trade places with someone else? Why?

Do you think everyone has something they don't like about themselves? Explain.

Kayla wanted to be skinny like her big sister. Do you think TV shows, movies, and magazines also tell us about how girls and boys should look? Do most people look that way in real life?

Does being rich, smart, thin, pretty, or handsome make a person happy? Why or why not?

"I'm not here for fun. . . . I'm here to win."

Was Kayla right to blame Ana, her teammate, when Kayla kicked the ball and missed the goal? Why or why not?

Do you participate in certain sports or activities to please yourself or to please others? Explain.

If you didn't win a game or weren't the best at some activity, would you want to quit? Why or why not?

Which do you think is more important—winning or having fun? Explain.

"Kayla was as close to perfect as anyone I knew, but I couldn't think of one thing that made her happy."

Do you think kids who are hard on themselves tend to be hard on others? Explain.

Do you think Kayla was more concerned about losing the game or disappointing her dad? Explain.

Is it okay to make mistakes? Why or why not?

What important lessons have you learned from your past mistakes?

"We need to celebrate who we are instead of complaining about who we aren't."

Why do you think people tend to focus more on what's wrong with them instead of what's right with them?

Which is more important—what you do or how you look?

What do you appreciate about your friends and family? Share your thoughts with them. If saying it out loud is uncomfortable, what other ways can you let them know?

Recommended Readings

For Young Children:

DeCesare, Angelo. *Anthony, the Perfect Monster*. New York: Random House, Beginner Books, 1996.

Graves, Keith. *Loretta: Ace Pinky Scout.* New York: Scholastic, 2007.

Manes, Stephen. *Be a Perfect Person in Just Three Days*. New York: Yearling, 1982.

Palmer, Pat. *Liking Myself*. San Luis Obispo: Impact Publishers, 1977.

For Tweens & Teens:

Adderholdt, Miriam, PhD, and Jan Goldberg. *Perfectionism: What's Bad About Being Too Good?* Minneapolis: Free Spirit Publishing, 1999.

Greenspon, Thomas, S. PhD. *What to Do When Good Enough Isn't Good Enough: The Real Deal on Perfectionism: A Guide for Kids*. Minneapolis: Free Spirit Publishing, 2007.

Rutledge, Jill Zimmerman, MSW, LCSW. *Picture Perfect: What You Need to Feel Better About Your Body*. Deerfield Beach: HCI Teens, 2007.

For Adults:

Basco, Monica Ramirez, PhD. *Never Good Enough: Freeing Yourself from the Chains of Perfectionism*. New York: Free Press, 1999.

Dweck, Carol, PhD. *Mindset: The New Psychology of Success*. New York: Random House, 2006.

Greenspon, Thomas S., PhD. *Freeing Our Families from Perfectionism*. Minneapolis: Free Spirit Publishing, 2002.

Mallinger, Allan E., MD, and Jeannette DeWyze. *Too Perfect: When Being in Control Gets Out of Control*. New York: Clarkson Potter, 1992.

Martin, Anthony M., PhD, and Richard P. Swinson, MD. *When Perfect Isn't Good Enough: Strategies for Coping with Perfectionism*. Oakland: New Harbinger Publications, 1998.

Martin, Courtney E. *Perfect Girls, Starving Daughters: The Frightening New Normalcy of Hating Your Body*. New York: Penguin Press, 2008.

Quindlen, Anna. *Being Perfect*. New York: Random House, 2005.

Sachs, Brad E., PhD. *The Good Enough Child: How to Have an Imperfect Family & Be Perfectly Satisfied*. New York: Harper Paperbacks, 2001.

To Ethyle and Rosemary,
two of the best role models a girl could ask for. —**T.J.L.**

This book is for my three best friends, and sisters,
Michele, Diane, and Christina. —**L.F.**

Text copyright © 2009 by Trudy Ludwig
Illustrations copyright © 2009 by Lisa Fields

Tricycle Press
an imprint of Ten Speed Press
PO Box 7123
Berkeley, California 94707
www.tricyclepress.com

Interior design by Tasha Hall
Cover design by Chloe Rawlins
Typeset in Mrs. Eaves
The illustrations in this book were rendered in oils and finished in Photoshop.

Library of Congress Cataloging-in-Publication Data
Ludwig, Trudy.
    Too Perfect / by Trudy Ludwig; illustrations by Lisa Field.
        p. cm.
    Summary: Maisie is convinced that her life would be much better if she were as "perfect" as her much-admired classmate Kayla until, after working together on a school project, she realizes that Kayla's perfectionism is not as wonderful as it seems. Includes information for parents.
    ISBN-13: 978-1-58246-258-5 (hardcover)
    ISBN-10: 1-58246-258-5 (hardcover)
    [1. Perfectionism (Personality trait)—Fiction. 2. Self-acceptance—Fiction. 3. Behavior—Fiction. 4. Schools—Fiction.] I. Field, Lisa, ill. II. Title.
    PZ7.L9763To 2009
    [Fic]—dc22
                                            2008020064

First Tricycle Press printing, 2009
Printed in China
1 2 3 4 5 6 – 13 12 11 10 09